THE LION KING

Adapted by Justine Korman
Illustrated by Don Williams and H. R. Russell

❦ A GOLDEN BOOK • NEW YORK

From the smallest ant to the largest elephant,
every living thing has a place in the great Circle of Life.
Mufasa's place was as king of the lions. Sarabi was the
queen. And their newborn cub, Simba, would one day
take his father's place as the Lion King.

But on this day, little Simba rested in the hands of the
wise baboon Rafiki, who sprinkled the cub with dust
and welcomed the future king to the great Circle of Life.

Mufasa's brother, Scar, did not attend the ceremony.
He was not happy that Simba was next in line to rule
the Pride Lands. For Scar had always wanted to be king.

Time passed, and Simba grew. Early one morning, Mufasa took him to the top of Pride Rock. "Simba, look," he said. "Everything the light touches is our kingdom."

"Wow!" the young lion said. Then he asked, "What about the shadowy place?"

"That's beyond our borders. You must never go there, Simba!" warned Mufasa.

Later Simba proudly told his uncle, Scar, "Someday
I'm gonna rule the whole kingdom! Well . . . everything
except the shadowy place. My father said
I can't go there."

"He's absolutely right," Scar slyly agreed. "An
elephant graveyard is no place for a young prince.
Only the bravest lions go there."

Scar knew Simba would want to prove that he was
brave. He said nothing as Simba ran off to ask his
friend Nala to explore the mysterious Shadow Lands
with him.

When the friends arrived at the Shadow Lands, they discovered an eerie, steamy place filled with elephant bones.

"It's so creepy," whispered Nala nervously.

"C'mon!" said Simba. "Let's check it out."

Zazu, the king's minister, had been looking for the cubs. When he caught up with them, he warned, "We are too far from the Pride Lands. It is dangerous!"

"Hee-hee-hee-hee-hee!" Strange laughter rang out. It belonged to three hyenas—Banzai, Shenzi, and Ed—who slinked out from an elephant skull.

When Zazu told the hyenas he was Mufasa's minister, they realized that Simba was the future king.

"He's a king fit for a meal," Banzai snickered. The hyenas chased Simba and Nala.

Suddenly a thunderous ROARRRR! rattled rocks and bones. It was the roar of Mufasa, the Lion King! The frightened hyenas ran away.

That evening Mufasa had a talk with Simba. "Being brave doesn't mean you go looking for trouble," he told his son.

"Dad," Simba asked suddenly, "we'll always be together, right?"

Mufasa gazed up at the sparkling heavens. "The great kings of the past look down on us from those stars," he said. "Whenever you feel alone, remember that those kings will always be there to guide you. And so will I."

Although Scar was angry with the hyenas for letting Simba go, he made a bargain with them. If they helped make him king, they could have the run of the Pride Lands.

So Scar brought Simba to a vast gorge and promised the cub a wonderful surprise if he would just wait on a certain rock. Scar then signaled to the hyenas.

The surprise turned out to be a stampeding herd of wildebeests, with the hyenas urging the herd on. The earth trembled. The wildebeests ran into the gorge, heading straight for Simba. He sought safety in a tree, but the branch bent under his weight.

Just before Simba would have fallen beneath the pounding hooves, Mufasa grabbed him and carried him to a rocky ledge. Then, through the thick, swirling dust, Simba saw his father disappear under the thundering herd.

When the stampede had passed, Simba found his father lying lifeless at the foot of a cliff. What Simba did not know was that Scar had pushed his brother off the rock!

"If it weren't for you, the king would still be alive," lied Scar, appearing at Simba's side.

"He tried to save me," said the cub, sobbing. "It was an accident."

"Run away, Simba," Scar advised. "Run away and never return."

Scar watched as Simba ran away. Then he sent his hyenas to kill the cub.

But when the hyenas reached a thorny thicket, they stopped. "He'll never survive in the desert," they reasoned. And so they returned to Pride Rock—and their new king, Scar.

Under the burning desert sun, Simba surely would
have died if it had not been for two curious creatures—
Timon the meerkat and Pumbaa the warthog.

Timon and Pumbaa felt sorry for the cub. They took him to their jungle home and taught him how to live by Timon's philosophy, *hakuna matata,* which meant "no worries." They also taught the cub to eat insects.

Simba tried to put the past behind him. But one clear night, the stars reminded him of the old kings and his father, Mufasa.

Then one day a lioness chased Pumbaa. Simba rushed to protect his friend.

"Nala!" he cried.

"Simba?" the lioness said. "I thought you were dead." The friends embraced. Then Nala told Simba that under cruel King Scar, the Pride Lands had become barren and the animals were starving. Hyenas were everywhere.

But Simba refused to go back and take his place as the Lion King. He did not feel worthy.

That night, wise old Rafiki found Simba alone. He led Simba to a small pool.

Simba saw his father's face in the water. Then he heard his father's voice. "Simba, look inside yourself," Mufasa said. "You are my son and the one true king. You must take your place in the Circle of Life."

So Simba set out for the Pride Lands to confront the false king. Later his friends Nala, Timon, and Pumbaa joined him.

"I'm surprised to see you alive," sneered Scar as Simba approached Pride Rock.

"I've come back to take my place as king," declared Simba.

With an angry snarl, Scar forced Simba to the edge of a cliff. As Simba struggled to hold on, Scar leaned down and whispered, "Here's my little secret, Simba. You didn't kill your father. I did."

Simba's heart filled with rage, and the strength of ten lions surged through him. He struggled up onto the rock, leaped on Scar, and the battle began!

Nala bravely led the other lionesses against the hyenas. Even Timon and Pumbaa joined the fight. The battle raged until all the hyenas ran from Pride Rock.

Simba chased Scar to the top of Pride Rock and cornered him.

Scar whimpered, "No. Please. Have pity on me."

"Run away, Scar," said Simba. "Run away and never return."

But when Simba turned his back, Scar attacked! Quick as the lightning that flashed above, Simba sent Scar flying over the cliff to the hungry hyenas below.

So Scar's evil reign ended, and Simba took his rightful place as the Lion King. In time, King Simba and Queen Nala had a cub of their own.

Way atop Pride Rock, their child rested in the hands of the wise baboon Rafiki, who sprinkled the cub with dust and welcomed her to the great Circle of Life.